Why Did the Underwear Cross the Road?

Gordon Korman

Why Did the Underwear Cross the Road?

SCHOLASTIC
HARDCOVER

Scholastic Inc.
New York

Library of Congress Cataloging-in-Publication Data

Korman, Gordon,
 Why did the underwear cross the road? / by Gordon Korman.
  p. cm.
 Summary: When Justin Zeckendorf is teamed up with two of the smartest girls in his fourth-grade class for a good deed contest, his zany ideas almost cost them their chance to win.

ISBN 0-590-47501-0

 [1. Schools — Fiction. 2. Contests — Fiction. 3. Helpfulness — Fiction.] I. Title.
PZ7.K8369Ti 1994
[Fic] — dc20   93-304231
                   CIP

12 11 10 9 8 7 6 5 4 3 2 1   4 5 6 7 8 9/9

Printed in the U.S.A.   37

Contents

Why Did the Underwear Cross the Road?

1

Tidal Wave Water Park

Oh, no!

Justin Zeckendorf slumped so low in his seat that his head banged on the desk. Mr. Carter was picking groups of three again. And Justin knew what that meant. He was going to get stuck with Margaret Zachary and Jessica Zander. It always worked out that way. They were the only three Z's in the fourth grade.

Justin felt a spitball bounce off his ear.

"Have fun, Dorf-head!" hissed a nasty voice from across the aisle. Byron Bigelow, the jerk. He was spitball champion of Spruce Valley Elementary, and probably the whole world. Byron wasn't going to have to be partners with Margaret and Jessica, the two most annoying girls in town. He would be put into Group 1, with the A's and B's.

With a sinking heart, Justin listened as the teacher went down the class list. "Anderson, Bigelow, Brown . . . Jordan, Markewicz, Newman . . . Stevens, Waldman, Young . . ." The teacher looked up and smiled. "And I guess our three Z's are together again."

"Zzzzz," buzzed Byron, and half the class joined in. The whole room vibrated. But did Mr. Carter notice? No!

"April is Good Deed Month in the city of Dover," the teacher announced brightly. "And Principal Ortiz has decided we're all going to be Good Samaritans. Do you know what that means?"

Instantly, Margaret's hand was in the air. "It means we do nice things to try to help others."

"It's from a Bible story," added Jessica. Jessica was always showing that she was as smart as Margaret, plus a tiny bit more.

"Zzzzz," buzzed Byron and several others.

Justin groaned. Now *he* would have to take the heat for Margaret and Jessica being a pair of know-it-alls — just because his name started with Z.

"Exactly," said Mr. Carter. "And I have something *very* exciting to announce. For every good deed, you earn points for your group. Mr. Ortiz will be taking the top group in every grade for a day at Tidal Wave Water Park."

Tidal Wave Water Park?! The words echoed inside Justin's head. Tidal Wave Water Park was just about the greatest place on the face of the earth. It had the Enormo-Slide, Dunk Mountain, and Splasherooski Whirlpool-o'-Fun! It was amazing! Or, at least, Justin thought it probably was. The Zeckendorfs never went to Tidal Wave Water Park because Justin's older brother, Trevor, caught a new germ every five minutes. When it got windy, Trevor got sick. When it got cold, Trevor ran a fever. When it got hot, Trevor had chills. At least once a week, Justin would come home from school to find his brother in his pajamas, coughing, sneezing, wheezing, and snorting. Nobody wanted to find out what would happen if Trevor got wet. So Tidal Wave Water Park was out.

But, hey! If Justin could win the Good Deed Contest, he'd get to go with Mr. Ortiz! It was the perfect chance! Maybe the only chance he'd ever get! He *had* to win! He *would* win! He could see himself rocketing down the Enormo-Slide in a shower of spray —

"Are we going to have to do good deeds for strangers?" came the soft voice of Jessica Zander. "I'm not allowed to talk to strangers."

Justin's daydream popped like a soap bubble. He had two partners in this thing — the two other Z's. How would he ever win with those *drips* dumping all over his great ideas?

"That brings up a very important point," approved Mr. Carter. "You should only go up to people you know, or people your parents say it's okay to talk to."

Justin set his jaw with determination. There was no way he was going to let Margaret Zachary and Jessica Zander cost him Tidal Wave Water Park. No way in the world!

2

A Blizzard of Underwear

"Hey, Jessica!" Justin ran up to her in the schoolyard at three-thirty that afternoon. "We have to have a meeting."

"What for?" asked Jessica suspiciously.

Justin stared. "What *for*? To figure out how we're going to win the trip to Tidal Wave Water Park!"

Jessica wrinkled her freckled nose. "Who wants to go to that dumb place? There's nothing but germs, germs, and more germs. If I get a rash, it could ruin my career!"

"What career?"

"My *acting* career! I've already been in four commercials, you know. Weren't you watching Channel 67 last night? I was in a five-second spot for the Handy-Dandy Radish Curler."

Justin made a face. "Well, let's all thank our lucky stars that we live in a world with curly radishes. Listen, Jessica — "

"Oh, Jessica — " Margaret Zachary arrived

on the scene. "What did you get on the spelling test?"

Justin could see Margaret's paper. It was marked 10 out of 10, A+.

Jessica held up her own test: 11 out of 10, A++. "I got perfect, too," she explained modestly, "but I put that *color* can also be spelled with a *u* if you're in England. So I got a bonus point."

Justin could almost see the smoke coming out of Margaret's ears. It drove Margaret crazy to be second-best at anything. That gave him an idea. If Margaret couldn't stand to be second-best at spelling, she probably felt the same way about good deeds. He turned to her. "What are we going to do about the big Contest?"

Margaret punched the air. "We're going to win it! Starting tonight, we'll all do the dishes at home, and take out the garbage. I'll walk my dog. . . ."

"I can't do anything that gets dirt under my fingernails," Jessica informed them. "I model my hands, you know. That was *my* finger that dialed the 900 number in the ad for the Santa's Wish List Hot Line."

Margaret ignored her. "And this weekend we can volunteer to cut our lawns, and clean out the attic, or maybe the garage — "

"Those aren't good deeds!" Justin interrupted. "That stuff's just a bunch of *chores!*"

"Just because they're your family doesn't mean you can't do things to help them out," lectured Margaret. "If we get our moms to write letters about all the good work we did, by Monday we'll be miles ahead of the other groups."

"Boy, are you guys ever lucky you've got me!" said Justin, shaking his head. "I'm an Idea Man. Why, just today I had this amazing idea."

Both girls looked at him skeptically.

"What if," Justin went on, "somebody dropped sixty million tons of instant mashed potatoes into Niagara Falls?"

Margaret blew her stack. "That's the stupidest thing I ever heard in my life! Where are you going to get that much mashed potatoes? And how are you going to get it to Niagara Falls? And who is it a good deed *for*?"

"And it's gross!" Jessica added.

"It's not a good deed," Justin replied impatiently. "I'm just showing you that I have totally original ideas. I bet no one's ever thought of that before. And it would probably work with instant oatmeal, too."

"We'll be kicked out of school," Jessica predicted darkly.

"Look," said Margaret, pointing down the street to the corner. "There's Mrs. Milarchuk. She must be on her way to the bus station. Let's give her a hand."

The Z's looked. At the crosswalk stood their neighbor, Mrs. Milarchuk, struggling under the weight of three large suitcases.

"Well, okay," said Justin grudgingly. "I'd rather rescue her from a burning building, but I guess we can help her to the bus station instead."

The three hurried over to perform their first good deed.

"Hi, Mrs. Milarchuk," greeted Margaret. "Can we help you with those?"

Before she could answer, Justin took charge. He ripped the suitcases from her hands, and divided them among the three partners. Then he grasped Mrs. Milarchuk by the arm, and marched her out into the middle of the street. The girls followed.

"But I'm not *going* to the bus station!" protested Mrs. Milarchuk.

Over the traffic noise, all Justin heard was *bus station*. "No need to thank us," he said cheerfully. "It's no trouble at all."

It was trouble for Jessica, who was finding it tough going with the heavy bag. "I can't do this," she announced in a strained voice. "If I get a hernia, it could ruin my career."

"What's wrong, Mrs. Milarchuk?" called Margaret. "You seem upset."

"I don't *want* to cross the street!" Mrs. Milarchuk exclaimed, struggling to free her arm from Justin's grip.

Justin looked at her peevishly. "You know, you're not supposed to fool around in the middle of the road."

At that moment, the light changed from green to red. Now, this could be dangerous! Without even thinking, Justin dropped the suitcase. Now he could use both hands to haul Mrs. Milarchuk to the safety of the opposite sidewalk. Margaret and Jessica retreated to the other side of the street.

"Why do you keep pushing me away?" Justin demanded, dragging her up the curb.

Her face glowed bright red. "Because I didn't *want* to cross the street! I wasn't *going* to the bus station! I was waiting for my son to pick me up!"

Justin looked surprised. "Why didn't you say so?"

"I *did* say so! I've been saying so ever since you kidnapped me!"

"Well," said Justin reasonably, "let's get you

9

back to the other side. Where's your suitcase?"

Mrs. Milarchuk's eyes bulged. "*You* had it!"

A scream came from Margaret across the street. "Justin, who left that suitcase in the middle of the road?"

He was about to run out and grab it when he saw the cement mixer — coming up fast!

KAPOW!

The suitcase bounced up like a Ping-Pong ball. It hit the pavement, and broke open. There was a blizzard of underwear.

Mrs. Milarchuk screamed as a pair of panty hose whizzed by on the antenna of a passing taxi.

The cement mixer's driver slammed on the brakes. Cars in all four directions screeched to a halt. Horns sounded, and shouts rang out.

"Hey, what's the holdup?"

"Move it along up there!"

"Who put this girdle in my windshield wipers?"

Margaret, Jessica, and several passersby were scrambling around, trying to gather up the clothing from the spilled suitcase.

Jessica snatched up a frilly pink camisole. "This reminds me of a riddle," she panted. "Why did the underwear cross the road? Give up? To get to the other side!"

A blue Plymouth pulled up, and a young man stuck his head out the driver's window. "Hey, Ma, whose stuff is blowing all over the street?"

A satin nightgown slithered silkily down a sewer opening.

Justin decided it was time to make his pitch. "Mrs. Milarchuk, could you please write a letter to our teacher explaining how much we helped you?"

"Aaaargh!"

3

A Great Big Humongous Good Deed

The big bulletin board was put up in the fourth-grade classroom. Mr. Carter went through all the groups, tallying up good deed points.

"And here's a letter from Mrs. Bigelow to let us know that Byron is feeding the O'Reillys' cat while they're on vacation. That's another point for Group 1."

Byron celebrated with a spitball down the collar of Justin's shirt.

"So Groups 1 and 3 are in first place with four points, with Group 6 close behind with three. A very solid start."

There was a knock at the door, and Mr. Ortiz, the principal, entered.

"Boys and girls, I have an announcement to make about the contest. Now, pay attention, because this is important. When you do a good deed for someone, always make sure that person wants your help. I've had a complaint from Mrs. Milarchuk. She said three of our students tried to force her across the road when she didn't want to go. And by the end of it, her suitcase was hit by a car!"

"That's totally untrue!" piped Margaret. "It was a cement truck!"

"The Z's did it!" came a stage whisper from Byron.

"Zzzzz," buzzed the class.

"Well," said the teacher after Mr. Ortiz had left, "I don't suppose we can award our three Z's any points for that."

"They should get negative numbers!" Byron called out.

"No fair!" cried Justin. "We haven't done negative numbers in math yet! How can you give us what we don't even understand?"

"*I* understand negative numbers," announced Margaret grandly.

GOOD DEED CONTEST

GROUP	I	II	III	IV	V	VI	VII	Z
POINTS	4	1	4	2	1	3	2	−5

The Z's held an emergency meeting at recess.

"Boy," said Justin. "I'm really disappointed in Mrs. Milarchuk. What a crab!"

"Yeah?" said Margaret. "How'd you like it if everybody in town got to see *your* underwear?"

"*See* it?" said Jessica. "Most of them drove *over* it! I hope no movie director saw me running after those size fifty-two bloomers and thought they were mine! That could cost me my career."

"It's all because of Mr. Ortiz!" Justin seethed. "He didn't even get our side of the story."

"We made idiots of ourselves, Justin," Margaret explained in her reasonable voice — the one that drove him crazy. "We don't have a 'side of the story.' "

"Mr. Ortiz is in a bad mood," Jessica supplied. "I heard his car was stolen last week."

Margaret was shocked. "His, too? That's the fourth one in just a couple of days! My uncle's Camaro disappeared right off his driveway in broad daylight. The paper says it's a ring of car thieves."

"That's fantastic!" Justin exclaimed.

Margaret frowned. "What's so great about getting your car stolen?"

Justin was quivering with excitement. "If we could catch the car thieves, *that* would be a

14

great big humongous good deed!"

"That's why we have police," Margaret pointed out. "So fourth graders don't have to solve crimes."

Justin was impatient. "You just don't think big. The other kids are getting points for cleaning their rooms and weeding the garden — stuff that doesn't help anybody. We have a chance to do something that helps everybody in town. We'll get twenty points — easy!" He glared at Margaret. "And we sure need a lot after you shot off your big mouth about understanding negative numbers. Now we're *negative!* Who knows how bad that could be?"

"Minus 5 just means that we're five points below zero," Jessica explained. "The next point we earn will make it minus 4."

That proved Jessica also understood negative numbers. *And* she could do math with them. Margaret looked displeased.

"Don't worry," Justin promised. "When we catch those car thieves, we'll be so far in first place that the other groups won't have a chance!"

4

Face-First in the Potato Salad

Justin looked up from his notebook. His eyes narrowed.

"Okay, Mr. Sullivan, where were you on the night of April second?"

The crossing guard shrugged. "I was at home."

"Ah, yes," said Justin, making notes. "But can you prove it?"

"My wife was with me."

"Not good enough," said Justin, shaking his head. "A wife might lie to protect her husband."

Suddenly, the crossing guard threw his hands up in the air. "All right, you got me! I tried to hide it, but you were too clever! I'm the car thief! I admit it! Arrest me!"

Margaret ran up, wide-eyed. "*Really,* Mr. Sullivan? *You're* the car thief?"

Mr. Sullivan dropped his hands and

laughed. "Of course not. I don't even drive. I was just helping Justin with the big investigation."

"I'm practicing," Justin explained. "So when we come face-to-face with the real crooks, I'll know what to say."

All at once, Jessica bustled onto the scene. Her face was bright red and streaked with tears. She was sobbing loudly, and dabbing at her eyes with a tissue.

"What's wrong?" chorused Mr. Sullivan and the other two Z's.

Instantly, the crying ended, and Jessica was all smiles. "I fooled you! You thought I was really crying!"

"What's the matter with you?" Margaret raged. "You scared us! We thought something terrible had happened!"

Jessica hugged herself joyfully. "Something did happen! Something great! Gregory Ashford is coming here to Dover!"

"Big deal," said Justin. "Who's Gregory Ashford?"

"Gregory Ashford, the famous Hollywood movie director!" Jessica shrieked. "Don't you know *anything*? He needs a nine-year-old girl to be in his next movie! And I have an audition!"

Mr. Sullivan stepped out into the street, and guided them to the other side. "That's terrific," he told Jessica. "Congratulations."

Justin frowned. "So if it's so good, why were you crying?"

"I was *rehearsing*," Jessica replied. "My character in the movie is named Clorinda. And Clorinda is sad a lot."

"This is ridiculous," said Margaret, annoyed. "You're being an actress, and Justin's being a detective, and nobody wants to hear about our next good deed."

"What good deed?" asked Justin.

"My mom's church raffle is in three days," Margaret beamed. "She's going to let us sell tickets right up until the night before the draw."

"That's not a good deed!" Justin exploded. "A good deed is catching a master criminal! Or fixing the hole in the ozone layer! Or making two countries do nuclear disarmament!"

"The money goes to charity," Margaret insisted. "And, remember, Group 6 got *two points* because Gracie sold out her tickets."

"It's not a bad idea," Justin decided grudgingly. "We'll work our way out of the negative numbers, then blow the other groups away when we catch the car thieves. I'd do anything to get to Tidal Wave Water Park!"

The raffle had a great prize — a twenty-eight-inch TV with a built-in VCR. It was something everybody wanted to win. So the three Z's were sold out of their thirty tickets on the first day.

Margaret was triumphant. "That was easy! I just wish we had more."

"We do," grinned Justin. He reached into his pocket and pulled out a thick stack of tickets.

The girls stared.

"Where did you get those?" asked Margaret, amazed. "Mom gave me the last thirty tickets they had!"

"I told you I was an Idea Man," said Justin smugly. "When I saw that sales were booming, I took my last ticket to my dad's office, and made these photocopies."

"You can't do that!" exclaimed Margaret. "They aren't real tickets!"

"They are *so* real tickets," Justin retorted. "If I didn't say they were copies, you never would have guessed. And they have as much chance to be winners as any of the others. Plus, it'll make more money for your mom's church group, *and* for charity. Besides" — his eyes gleamed — "if selling thirty tickets is worth two points, then selling ninety tickets should get us *six*."

"We'd be out of the negative numbers," said Margaret breathlessly.

"We'd even have one point to build on," added Jessica.

Margaret took the tickets from Justin, and riffled through them. Justin was right. They were exactly like the real thing. They had stubs and everything, so the buyers had the same chance to win as everyone else. They were even printed on the same kind of yellow paper. And it *was* for charity. . . .

"What are we waiting for?" asked Justin. "Let's start selling!"

The raffle was a huge success. Mrs. Zachary and her committee were a little puzzled, though. It seemed that they had raised *more* money than there had been tickets to sell.

"Oh, it must have been people making donations on top of the price of their tickets," decided Mrs. Abernathy, the president of the Ladies' Auxiliary. "How nice."

Saturday night was the big drawing. Margaret nagged Justin and Jessica into attending the buffet supper in the church hall.

"This is a waste of time," Justin complained. "As soon as your mom writes the letter to Mr. Carter, our six points are in the bag. We should be concentrating on our investigation." He looked down at his paper plate and grimaced. "Besides, I wouldn't feed this potato salad to a sewer rat."

"I'll have you know the potato salad was made by *my mother*," said Margaret sternly. "And it's *delicious!*"

"I should be home rehearsing," put in Jessica.

"How are you going to be in a whole movie?" Margaret demanded. "It takes you three weeks to learn to say, 'Mom, the sink's backed up,' for a Drāno commercial!"

"That shows how much *you* know!" sneered Jessica. "I had to think back to times in my life when our sink really *was* backed up. That way I could say it with true feeling. The lines are nothing; it's the *emotion*."

Justin snapped his fingers. "If she gets to be Clorinda in that movie, maybe we can wangle some points out of it."

"How?" asked Margaret. "It's not a good deed."

"It'll be great P.R. for our school," Justin reasoned. "You know, she can go on TV with Gregory What's-his-face . . ."

"Gregory Ashford *never* goes on TV," Jessica interrupted. "He's a true artist. He won't even let anybody take his picture."

"He sounds like a goofball to me," said Justin sourly. "Who passes up a chance to go on TV?"

Aside from the bad-tasting potato salad, the hall was hot, and the speeches were long and boring. More than once Justin felt his eyelids drooping. So he kept himself awake by scanning the faces in the crowd. There were quite a few people who had bought their tickets from him. His mind raced. Wouldn't it be great if one of his customers was the winner? Maybe the Z's could squeeze out some extra points for selling the winning ticket. Maybe he could help the guy carry the prize home for even *more* points! And what if the winner dropped the television set on his toe, and Justin could assist the doctor who would perform the microsurgery? That could rocket the Z's into first place! They might not even need to catch the car thieves —

"Justin! Justin, wake up!" Margaret was

shaking his shoulder. "They're doing the drawing!"

From a revolving Plexiglas drum filled with tickets, Mrs. Abernathy pulled a single stub.

"And the grand prize of a twenty-eight-inch television set with a built-in VCR goes to the holder of ticket number . . . 2406!"

"*I won!*" came a chorus of many voices. Twenty-two people got up and rushed onto the stage, waving their tickets. They all seemed to notice each other at the same time.

"*You* won?! *I* won!"

In horror, Mrs. Abernathy checked ticket after ticket. "Oh, dear!" she said faintly. "You all seem to have number 2406! How could this happen?"

Margaret went white to the ears. She grabbed Justin by the collar. "When you photocopied all those tickets — did you remember to change the numbers?"

Justin looked blank. "No. Why?"

"Because sixty people just won the same television set!"

"Sixty-*one* people," said Jessica thoughtfully. "You're forgetting the real ticket he copied from."

It finally hit Justin. All those photocopied

tickets had the same number! And that number was 2406!

One winner tried to pick up the television set. But the others thought he shouldn't have it. In no time, a tug-of-war broke out by the revolving drum. There was a lot of pushing and shoving until the first man lost his balance and fell off the stage. He landed on the buffet table, face-first in the potato salad.

"I'm suing!" he screamed and marched out of the building, raining white slop.

Angry shouts filled the hall.

"Boy," said Justin. "It's a good thing all sixty-one didn't show up tonight! We could have a riot on our hands!"

"This is all your fault!" wailed Margaret.

"Will you shut up?" hissed Justin. "No one's going to know it was us!"

GOOD DEED CONTEST

GROUP	I	II	III	IV	V	VI	VII	Z
POINTS	7	3	6	3	2	5	4	−10

"Zzzzz!" Byron Bigelow led the buzzing.

"What a rip-off!" grumbled Justin. "This wasn't worth *five whole points*! Like it's *our fault* the church couldn't afford enough TV's for all the winners!"

"They had to cancel everything and refund the money," said Margaret. "They're doing it over, but no one wants to buy any tickets this time."

"I wouldn't, either," said Justin. "They give a lousy raffle. And the nerve of that Mrs. Abernathy, complaining about us to Mr. Ortiz."

Jessica spoke up. "My brother heard that the man who got thrown into the potato salad is suing for whiplash."

Margaret was outraged. "Whiplash? How can he have whiplash?"

Jessica shrugged. "He doesn't, really. But you're not allowed to sue for potato salad."

Margaret put her hands on her hips. "We're in big trouble! *Now* will you two start listening to me?"

"Are you kidding?" cried Justin. "We need ten points to get back to *zero* — another seven to catch up to Group 1! If there was ever a time for an Idea Man, this is it!"

And throughout all this, the class was buzzing at the unfortunate Z's.

5

Doctor Dog

CHAPTER 5: GRAND THEFT AUTO
Almost all stolen cars are sold in other
states. The good detective is always on the
lookout for suspicious drivers of cars with out-
of-state license plates.

"Justin!"

Mr. Carter snatched away Justin's science book. Behind it everyone could now see *101 Detective Tips*.

"Hey, Mr. Detective, here's a clue!" A Byron Bigelow spitball bounced off the end of Justin's nose.

Mr. Carter frowned at Justin. "Since you're paying attention *so well*, maybe you can tell us the name of a dinosaur that doesn't eat meat."

Justin gulped. "Uh — Pasta-saurus?"

The class was still laughing when the bell went off at three-thirty.

"Hey, Justin," said Jessica in annoyance.

"Quit cracking jokes in class. How am I supposed to practice being Clorinda when everybody's laughing? Clorinda is a very serious person."

"I wasn't joking," Justin defended himself.

"Then that's even worse," said Margaret. "That means you think there's really such a thing as Pasta-saurus! What's next? Linguinadon? Pizza-ceratops? You're giving our group a bad name!"

"When we catch those car thieves, we'll be heroes." Suddenly, Justin froze. "Look at that!" He pointed to a shiny white Pontiac in a long row of vehicles parked at the curb.

"It's a car. So what?" replied Margaret. "It's no different from any of these others."

Justin's eyes gleamed. "Yes it is! Look at the license plate! It's from New York State! The book says to watch for out-of-state plates!" Cautiously, he approached the open window on the driver's side.

"What are you doing?" asked Margaret.

Justin squinted at the papers lying on the passenger's seat. "Look — a rental contract! This is a Rent-a-Car!" He craned his neck. "I can't make out the driver's name."

"Get away from there, Justin!" exclaimed Margaret. "This isn't your car!"

But Justin leaned further into the open window, determined to learn the name of the driver. "Are you kidding?" he replied, his voice strained with effort. "This guy's a suspect! I've never had a real suspect before!" His feet swung up off the pavement.

Jessica was worried. "I don't know what we're doing, but I'm pretty sure we're not allowed to be doing it."

Justin balanced on his stomach, his head and shoulders in the car, his legs waving in the air.

All at once, a big brown-and-white Saint Bernard leaped up from the floor of the back seat. With a joyous bark, the giant dog dealt Justin's face a juicy lick. Shocked, Justin tumbled forward into the car. The dog climbed on top of him, slopping its long tongue all over the fourth-grader's face.

"Help!" came Justin's muffled cry.

His fellow Z's sprang to the rescue. Each girl grabbed a foot and pulled. The shoes and socks came off.

"Hey, you kids!" bellowed a foghorn voice. A wild-eyed man in an expensive suit rushed out of the Hotel Dover, waving his arms and shouting. "Get away from that car!" He barged past Margaret and Jessica and hauled Justin

out by his bare feet. "What were you doing in there?"

"Oh, nothing," said Justin, gathering up his shoes and socks. "By the way, sir, where were you on the night of April second?"

"Mind your own business!" stormed the man.

Margaret walked over to the car and patted the Saint Bernard, who was hanging his big head out the window, panting and drooling. "He's so friendly. What's his name?"

The man was growing angrier. "He doesn't have a name!" he shouted. "He's just my dog, okay? *My dog!*"

"My dog," mused Margaret. "M.D."

"Like a doctor," put in Jessica.

"Right!" Margaret snapped her fingers. "We'll call him Doctor Dog!" The animal perked up and licked her hand. "See? He likes it!"

The man tore at his hair. "You're not going to call him anything! You kids have a lot of nerve! You crawl around my car like it was a jungle gym in a public playground!"

"Sorry, mister — " Margaret began.

"Get away from my dog!" He grasped the Saint Bernard's collar and yanked it away from Margaret. "There's nothing I hate worse than other people messing with my stuff!"

"Sir," Justin persisted, "where were you on the night of — ?"

"Leave me alone!" The man stuffed himself into the Pontiac. Then he squealed away, leaving the three Z's standing in a cloud of burning rubber.

Justin kicked on his sneakers. "He could be our man."

Margaret snorted. "Just because he's crabby doesn't mean he's the car thief."

Justin smiled importantly. "I got a look at the rental contract. Guess what the guy's name is — John Smith!"

"So?" asked Jessica.

"It's a fake name!" Justin exclaimed excitedly. "Nobody is named Smith *really*! He rented that car under another name because he doesn't want anybody to know who he is. Maybe the cops are after him!"

"You're crazy," said Margaret positively. "My mother's maiden name is Smith, and she *definitely* wasn't running away from the police! It's time to give up these stupid schemes of yours and concentrate on some *real* good deeds, Justin. Justin? Are you listening to me?"

But Justin was already leafing through *101 Detective Tips*.

6

A Thousand Pieces of Shredded Toilet Paper

The Z's held their next meeting at Justin's house. They sat around the kitchen table, listening to the coughs and sneezes coming from down the hall. Trevor Zeckendorf, Justin's older brother, was working on his ninth cold of the year.

"Would anyone like some cookies?" asked Mrs. Zeckendorf, pouring three glasses of milk.

"I shouldn't get fat," declined Jessica. "Clorinda is very skinny."

Mrs. Zeckendorf put a plate of pecan clusters down in the middle of the table. "How are you kids doing in the Good Deed Contest?"

"Oh, fantastic," said Justin.

After Mrs. Zeckendorf had left the kitchen, Margaret turned on Justin. "How can you lie like that to your own mother?"

"It's not a lie," said Justin through clenched

teeth. "It's going to be the truth. We've already got our suspect."

"Mr. Smith is not a suspect," Margaret explained in her know-it-all voice. "If he's this super-dangerous car thief, how come he isn't hiding out? He just walked up to us on the street."

"That's part of his fiendish plan," Justin argued. "He *acts* like a normal person so no one suspects that he's really a fugitive from justice."

"He's just a little cranky, that's all," Margaret insisted. "I love his dog, though."

"*Doctor* Dog," corrected Jessica.

"That's a criminal's dog!" said Justin, horrified. "He could be a trained killer!"

"Oh, sure," laughed Margaret. "He almost licked you to death."

"I could have suffocated!" Justin protested. "It was an attack! That's why we have to be extra careful when we start gathering proof against Mr. Smith."

"How do we do that?" asked Jessica, bored.

"I'm only up to Chapter 5," Justin admitted. " 'Evidence' is Chapter 7. And it takes forever to read. Hardly any pictures."

"Look," said Margaret, "I've got a *real* idea. It's spring."

"So?" said Justin. "You think Mr. Smith is going to give us a signed confession because we know what season it is?"

"This has nothing to do with stolen cars," Margaret persisted. "It's a new good deed. Everybody's windows are dirty from all the rain. We can wash them."

"Okay," sighed Justin reluctantly. "Until I make it through Chapter 7, we may as well get some points in the meanwhile."

They started with Justin's next-door neighbors. Mr. and Mrs. Chisholm weren't at home, but their teenage son, Randy, answered the door.

"What?" he mumbled.

"Hi, Randy," Margaret greeted. "We're here to see if you want your windows washed."

"How much?"

"Nothing," Margaret replied with a toothy smile. "It's a good deed."

"No."

"*No?!*" Justin exploded. "What do you mean, *no*? It's free! All you have to do is write a note to our teacher! We'll even tell you what to put!"

"No," repeated Randy, and slammed the door on them.

Justin made a face at Margaret. "Way to go."

Margaret shrugged. "It's not my fault he said no."

Shouldering the squeegee like a rifle, Justin led them down the street. "We do the next place *my* way."

At the McClintocks' house, he took charge. Rather than going up to the door, he unfurled the garden hose from the side of the garage.

"What are you doing?" hissed Margaret.

"If you knock on their door," Justin explained, pulling the hose around to the front, "you're giving them a chance to say no. We're going to wash the windows *first*. Then we ring the doorbell, and show them what a great job we did." He turned to Jessica, who was stationed by the outdoor tap. "Let 'er rip!"

An arc of water shot from the end of the hose. But instead of splashing against the glass, it sailed straight in the open window.

"Stop it! Stop it!" shrieked Margaret. "The window's open! You're flooding their house!" Desperately, she tried to wrestle the hose out of Justin's hand. Instead of turning off the tap, Jessica rushed over to help Margaret. The three struggled in the spray, until Margaret broke free. She turned off the water.

"I'm soaked to the skin!" breathed Jessica in horror. "I'm going to have a scratchy throat for my audition with Gregory Ashford!"

Justin and Margaret rushed over to the window and looked inside. There was a huge puddle in the middle of the polished hardwood floor. It led to a big wet spot on the Chinese rug. The couch dripped. A large flowering cactus lay on its side, bowled over by the force of the hose.

"We've got to *do* something!" whispered Margaret.

"Right!" agreed Justin. "Let's get out of here!"

"That's not what I mean!" said Margaret sternly. "This is our fault, and we've got to own up." She headed for the front door and reached up to ring the bell.

Horrified, Justin sprinted over and put an iron grip on her arm. "Are you *crazy*? If this gets back to Mr. Carter, we'll be slapped with more negative numbers! And then we'll *never* make it to Tidal Wave Water Park!"

"Then you can go for a swim in the McClintocks' living room," said Margaret coldly. "It's wetter." She pulled her arm free and rang the bell.

Jessica sniffled, and wrung out the hem of her skirt. "I think I'm getting a scratchy throat *right now*!"

35

"Sssssh!" cautioned Margaret.

The three Z's waited. There was no answer.

Justin threw his arms up in victory. "Hooray!" he exclaimed. "They're not home! We can dry off their living room, and they'll never know what happened!"

"But how?" protested Margaret. "We can't get inside till the McClintocks come home."

Justin rolled his eyes. "What got us into this mess in the first place? *The window's open!*"

Margaret was horrified. "You can't just climb into their house! It's against the law!"

"I've been in there a million times," Justin argued, leading them back to the window. "My mom and I watered their plants for them when they went to Bermuda."

Justin hoisted himself over the sill and dropped inside. As soon as his wet sneakers hit the puddle, his feet shot out from under him. He crashed to the floor.

The girls scrambled in after him.

"Justin — " Margaret hissed. "Are you all right?"

Jessica interrupted his answer. *"Oh, no!"* she whispered, pointing. "Someone's *home!*"

The cellar door was open, and the light was on downstairs. Justin crept over and peered around the doorframe. The girls peered timidly, one over each shoulder.

Down in the basement, Mr. and Mrs. McClintock reclined in beanbag chairs. Each wore a giant set of headphones hooked up to their stereo.

Relieved, Justin laughed out loud. Margaret put a finger to her lips, terrified.

"They can't hear us," grinned Justin. "The McClintocks are nuts about opera music. But they play it so loud, the neighbors complain. One time my dad thought someone was being tortured in here because of all the screaming. So now they wear earphones." He chuckled. "Wait here."

He darted into the kitchen. When he returned, his arms were loaded with paper towels.

The three Z's got down on their hands and knees and began sopping up the puddles. Following Justin's lead, the girls tossed the wet paper out the window. They worked furiously, scrubbing and drying. "What if the opera ends?" quavered Jessica.

"No way!" scoffed Justin, wringing out a corner of the Chinese rug. "Those things *never* end. They'll be in earphones for hours." His mind wandered. What if those headphones weren't really headphones? What if they were *electrodes* — and the McClintocks were victims of some evil brainwashing experiment? Wouldn't it be great if the three Z's could rescue them? What a good deed that would be!

His daydream was interrupted by Margaret's frantic whisper. "We're out of paper towels!"

They finished off the rug with Kleenex. But the couch was still soaking, and all that was left was half a roll of toilet paper from the main floor bathroom.

They set to work again, sopping and scrubbing. The dark velvet couch was drying well, but the floral tissue seemed to fall apart on contact. Clumps of pink pulp stood out like polka dots against the fabric.

"We can't leave it like this!" gasped Margaret.

"Why not?" demanded Justin. "It looks fine to me."

"You think they're not going to notice a thousand pieces of shredded toilet paper?"

Justin sighed. "Oh, all right. I'll get the vacuum cleaner."

Jessica came to life. "They'll hear us!"

"Are you kidding?" snapped Justin. "They wouldn't hear an air raid through those earphones!" He ran out into the hall and reappeared with a full-size upright vacuum. He plunked it onto the sofa and ran to plug it in.

"Justin, *don't!*" Margaret squeaked. "The couch is — "

ZAP!

" — wet!"

A shower of sparks shot out of the vacuum cleaner. The short circuit blew every fuse in the house. The clock on the wall stopped ticking. The basement light went out.

Margaret went white as a ghost. Her fellow Z's understood at once. Without electricity, there was no stereo.

"Must be a power failure," came a voice from below. This was followed by the sound of footsteps on the basement stairs.

"*Hide!*" rasped Justin. He grabbed the vacuum cleaner and hustled it back to the hall closet. Then he crammed the vacuum, Margaret, Jessica, and finally himself inside. He pulled the door shut just in time.

The golf bag fell on them first. Then Margaret accidentally touched the button that opened up a giant umbrella. But it was the hissing sound that made Justin nervous. For he had stepped on the release pin of Mr. McClintock's army surplus inflatable lifeboat. With a *sssss*, the big yellow raft filled with air.

The three Z's were pinned up against the walls, the door, and each other.

"We're dead!" quavered Jessica.

"Not yet!" whispered Justin.

"I'll check the fuse box," came Mr. McClintock's voice from out in the hall. "Honey, where's the flashlight?"

"In the front closet, dear," was the reply.

"*Now* we're dead," Justin amended.

Mr. McClintock opened his closet door. The contents exploded out at him — a vacuum cleaner, golf clubs, an umbrella, a lifeboat, and three Z's.

7

The Fourth-Grade Wrecking Crew

"I hate you, Justin Zeckendorf!"

Justin stared at Jessica. "Me? What did I do?"

"I was rehearsing Clorinda in front of my parents," the young actress pouted. "And right in the middle of everything, I sneezed, because *you* made me get a scratchy throat! I hate your guts!"

Then she spilled the beans about the Mc-Clintocks' living room in front of the whole class. So when the three Z's were called to the office, there was no mystery about it.

The principal was very angry. "Every other group in every other grade is doing just fine! We've got kindergartners running errands and carrying parcels without so much as a single incident! And *you* have become the fourth-grade wrecking crew! What do you have to say for yourselves?"

"We're sorry," mumbled Margaret and Jessica in unison.

Justin's mind was somewhere else. "Mr. Ortiz, when we go to Tidal Wave Water Park, do they have changing rooms? Or do you have to wear your bathing suit under your clothes?"

They were kicked out of the office.

Justin was disgusted. "I can't believe Mr. McClintock ratted us out! He used to be so cool!"

Margaret scowled at him. "People usually get less cool when you trash their living room!"

They entered Mr. Carter's classroom. The bulletin board greeted them:

GOOD DEED CONTEST

GROUP	I	II	III	IV	V	VI	VII	Z
POINTS	9	4	8	6	4	8	6	−15

"Zzzzz!"

CHAPTER 7: EVIDENCE
No person can be convicted of a crime without evidence to prove he is guilty. The good detective must be patient. Only when there is proof can an arrest be made.

42

It was afternoon recess. Justin sat on a flat rock at the edge of the playground. He was reading his detective book while trying to ignore a noisy dodgeball game. As usual, Byron Bigelow was the loudest and the most obnoxious. Justin tried to return to his reading.

Part 1: Fingerprints

WHAM!

The ball caught him full in the face, knocking him backwards into a tulip bed.

"Oops," said Byron, grinning.

Mud from head to toe, Justin jumped up, ready to do battle.

"What's going on here?" came the voice of Ms. Wu, the teacher on yard duty. "Justin, go and get yourself cleaned up."

Fuming, Justin trudged to the Boys' Room and washed up as best he could. He emerged just as the bell rang to end recess. So he was the first one back to class.

There was a note sitting on Mr. Carter's desk. Justin thought he'd better take a peek at it, just in case it had anything to do with the Z's.

Mr. Carter,

Been thinking about our problems with your Z's & g. deed contest. How about using your groups as coaches for kindergarten field day Apr. 25? Will count as g. deed for everybody, okay? It's so easy, even your Z's might get it right & at least we can keep an eye on them.

Mr. Ortiz

Margaret and Jessica appeared in the doorway, deep in conversation.

"So," Margaret was saying, "how long was your story for English? I wrote eight pages."

"Oh, wow," replied Jessica. "Mine's only seven. Of course, that's not including the pop-up illustrations — "

"The stupidest thing that could have happened just happened!" Justin interrupted. He showed them the note from Mr. Ortiz. "Can you believe it? Our investigation is going into high gear, and now we have to drop everything and baby-sit a bunch of five-year-olds!"

Margaret scanned the letter. "Our principal hates us!" she exclaimed in horror.

"He doesn't hate us," Jessica pointed out. "He just thinks we're idiots."

"Oh, so that's *way* better!" Margaret said sarcastically. All at once she snapped to attention. "Wait a minute! Kindergarten field day counts as a good deed! It's a chance to get points. If we win the contest, maybe Mr. Ortiz will like us again."

"Even if they give us a *hundred* points," argued Justin, "everyone else will be getting the same amount, so we'll still be behind the other groups." He paused, thinking. "Unless — "

"It's his Idea Man face," Jessica warned.

"If our kindergartners win all the events, all the games, all the ribbons, and all the prizes, and have the most fun," Justin suggested, "then *we'll* get the credit for it. *And* extra points."

"But our group might turn out to be a bunch of lumps," Margaret pointed out. "We can't *make* Mr. Carter give us only the fastest runners and the best athletes."

"That's why we'll have to train them," Justin replied.

"Train *who*?" asked Jessica. "We won't

know till the twenty-fifth who's going to be in our group."

"You guys are so smart, but you don't *think*!" exclaimed Justin. "How come the three of us are always together? Alphabetical order! We *are* the last group, so we'll *get* the last group."

8

In Training

Justin stepped out of the fourth-grade class, shutting the door quietly behind him. He took a few steps toward the bathroom, then doubled back. He tiptoed past the office to the music room. A hodgepodge of crashing, clanging, and dingling met his ears. Carefully, he raised his head and peered in the small window in the door. Perfect. The kindergartners were busy with rhythm band.

He dashed to the empty kindergarten area and padded inside. There on Ms. Dollop's desk was the class list — twenty-four students, exactly the same as Mr. Carter's fourth grade.

Instantly, Justin's eyes skipped to the bottom of the paper.

Tuppleman, Seth
Vernon, Nicolette
Yastremski, Harvey

At recess, the three Z's gathered their kindergarten team and steered them to a quiet corner of the schoolyard.

Seth Tuppleman, age five, was almost in tears. He worked up his nerve and faced Justin and the girls. "Are you going to beat us up?"

"Of course not!" exclaimed Margaret. "You're our team for field day. We have to have a meeting."

Nicolette Vernon pointed to the schoolyard. Her classmates were involved in a game of tag. "Nobody else is having a meeting. I want to go play."

"Sorry, no playing," said Justin. "You're in training."

"Training?" repeated Harvey Yastremski. "For field day?"

"Right," Justin confirmed. "Don't you want a chest full of ribbons and a bag full of prizes? And when people look at you, don't you want them to say, 'There's the guy who grabbed the gusto on field day?' "

"Hey, yeah!" Harvey piped up. "Let's do training!" He paused. "What's training?"

"We're going to turn you into a lean, mean, field day machine," Justin promised. "All the gold medal events — the egg-and-spoon race, the fifteen-yard dash, tee-ball, the three-legged relay, the beanbag throw, red rover — you're going to win it all!"

Jessica looked at Justin sternly. "This isn't right. You're putting too much pressure on these poor little kids — "

But Seth, Harvey, and Nicolette were already cheering.

"We're gonna *kill* those other teams!" roared Harvey.

"Kick some serious butt!" added Nicolette.

"We're not getting beaten up!" cheered Seth.

"This is all top secret," Justin added. "You can't tell anybody you're in training."

"Not even our families?" asked Seth.

"*Especially* not your families," said Justin. "Parents might call Mr. Ortiz, and then we're dead. Now," he said, all business, "when do your folks leave you totally on your own?"

The three kindergartners just stared at him. "Never," they chorused.

Justin looked totally bewildered. "Never?"

"Oh, Justin, don't be such a dope!" Margaret exploded. "They're *five years old!*"

"I suppose *you* got to go bungee-jumping off Mount Everest when you were in kindergarten," Jessica said sarcastically.

"But how are we going to train them if we can't get their parents off their backs?" Justin complained.

Seth mustered up his nerve. "Nicolette and I go to After-School Club at three-thirty."

Justin was impatient. "What's After-School Club?"

"It's just fourth and fifth graders helping to look after the younger students until their parents get off work," Jessica explained.

Justin looked mildly interested. "Do you get paid?"

"Of course not," replied Margaret. "But they have milk and cookies for you in the library."

Justin rolled his eyes. "Big fat hairy deal."

Margaret was angry. "How dare you look down on milk and cookies, Justin Zeckendorf? Milk and cookies build strong bones and a healthy body. Schoolkids in this country have been eating milk and cookies for two hundred years!"

Justin groaned. "Okay, it's settled. We help with After-School Club, choke down the stupid milk and cookies, and head outside for some major training."

Harvey spoke up. "What about me? I'm not in After-School Club. I have to walk home with my brother, Kevin."

"Well," sighed Justin. "We'll just have to cut a deal with Kevin."

Kevin Yastremski wasn't out for recess with the other fifth graders. The three Z's caught up with him in the library. He was at a long table, writing four hundred lines of *I will not talk in class.*

"So you want me to hang out every day while you train my kid brother." He scowled. "What's in it for me?"

"You get to see Harvey winning all those ribbons — " Justin began.

Kevin cut him off. "That's what's in it for Harvey. What's in it for me?"

"But we don't have anything to give you," said Margaret.

"Sure we do," Justin amended. "How about free milk and cookies every day at three-thirty?"

The fifth grader laughed in his face. "In your dreams, Zeckendorf! Milk and cookies! What a joke!"

Justin's face flamed red. "I'll have you know," he said with dignity, "that milk and cookies build strong bones and a healthy body. Schoolkids in this country have been eating milk and cookies for two hundred years, and

51

I have that on the highest authority!"

Kevin held out a beefy hand. "It's a deal."

At the end of the day, Justin, Margaret, and Jessica officially signed on as helpers for the After-School Club.

While Justin slipped cookies and milk through the open library window to Kevin, Margaret piped up, "Who wants to go outside?"

Harvey, Nicolette, and Seth charged out the door, followed by Jessica and Margaret. Justin brought up the rear. It was time for training to begin.

His ramrod-straight arm balancing the spoon and egg, Harvey bustled across the jump rope that marked the finish line.

Margaret clicked her stopwatch. "Excellent!" she cheered. "You've cut three-tenths of a second off your time!"

Justin was rubbing liniment on Nicolette's right shoulder. "To be a true beanbag champion," he explained, "you have to take perfect care of your arm. One sore muscle can be the difference between finishing first or finishing last."

Seth was chinning himself on a low bar in

the jungle gym. " . . . 8 . . . 9 . . . 10!" He jumped to the floor. There stood Jessica, fists clenched. She was moaning her agony to the sky.

Seth's lower lip quivered. "I'm sorry! I promise I'll do better next time!" He burst into tears. "I'm a failure! I let you down — "

Instantly, Jessica was all smiles. "No, no — I'm not mad. Clorinda is."

Seth was wide-eyed. "Who's Clorinda?"

"Clorinda isn't a real person," Jessica explained. "That's the part I'm trying out for in the new Gregory Ashford film."

Seth was impressed. "Are you a movie star?"

Jessica looked disappointed. "Don't you recognize me? You know — from the TV commercial for Smell-away Foot Odor Pads? I'm the girl who fainted when the actor took off his shoe."

"That's my favorite commercial!" Seth exclaimed, delighted. "Wow! You're famous!"

"Sort of," Jessica admitted modestly.

Justin called the group together. "Great workout, guys! What's the word?"

"Victory!" chorused the three kindergartners.

9

Watching the Cement

It was Saturday morning, and Margaret and Jessica were heading for Spruce Valley Elementary School. The school steps were being repaired that day, and Margaret had a plan.

"If we keep listening to Justin, we'll never get out of the negative numbers. It's up to you and me."

Jessica looked doubtful. "We're supposed to be a group. Maybe we shouldn't do good deeds without him."

"Every time we do what he says, we end up in trouble," Margaret argued. "He thinks Mr. Smith is a car thief! He thinks Doctor Dog is a killer! He wants to turn Niagara Falls into mashed potatoes!"

"That *was* pretty weird," Jessica admitted.

At the school, they marched up to Mr. Angelino, the custodian. He was watching over the work crew.

"Good morning, sir," said Margaret pleasantly. "We volunteer."

Mr. Angelino looked blank. "For what?"

"You know the Good Deed Contest," Margaret explained. "We help you, and you write a letter to Mr. Carter, and we get points."

The custodian snapped his fingers. "Right! The big contest. Some first graders have been helping me pick up litter. Cute little guys. They've already got fourteen points. But I guess you older kids have a lot more than that."

"The competition is nowhere near us," gritted Margaret.

It was the truth. The three Z's needed fifteen points to reach zero, and four more than that to move into a last-place tie.

Jessica spoke up. "I'm not allowed to use a chainsaw. Or to get dirt under my fingernails. Or to climb any ladders, or stand where somebody might drop a brick on my head. And I'm not allowed to drive the hydraulic crane."

Mr. Angelino stared at her. "We don't have a hydraulic crane. We're just cementing the front steps. In fact," he added, "I really don't think there's anything for you to do here. Sorry."

"Oh, please!" piped Margaret. "We *really* want to do a good deed!"

"Well . . ." The custodian's eyes fell on the

large cement mixing tray that stood nearby. "I know." He led them over to it, and pointed at the freshly mixed concrete. "That's your job. You stand right here and watch the cement."

"And that'll be a big help?" Jessica asked uncertainly.

"Of course," grinned Mr. Angelino. "Good luck."

"You can depend on us," vowed Margaret.

They sat in complete silence, never taking their eyes from the tray.

"Pssst!"

Both girls stared. There stood a short figure in a broad-brimmed hat that was pulled down low over dark glasses. He was wrapped in an oversized trench coat that dragged along the ground.

"Pssst! It's me!" A hand reached up and raised the sunglasses. It was Justin.

"Justin!" cried Margaret. "Why are you dressed like that?"

"Shhh!" Justin cautioned. "I'm doing a stakeout."

"What's that?" asked Jessica.

"It's Chapter 8 in my detective book. I'm in disguise so I can follow Mr. Smith."

"What for?" asked Margaret.

"To see where he goes, of course!" Justin

exclaimed. "He could lead me to the stolen cars!"

"So what are you doing *here*?" asked Jessica.

Justin looked sheepish. "Stakeouts are kind of boring. It's been almost ten minutes, and he hasn't even come out of the hotel! Plus, the book doesn't say anything about how you can go to the bathroom without stopping the stakeout."

"We're helping the work crew," Margaret informed him. "It's a very important good deed."

Justin frowned. "It looks like you're just standing here."

Margaret bristled. "That shows what *you* know. We're watching the cement."

"Why? Do you expect it to get up and leave?"

The girls stared at him. They had no answer.

Justin gave a great hoot of laughter. "How come you two get straight A's, and *I'm* stupid? You don't have to watch cement! It just sits there!"

Margaret's face was burning red. "Okay, Mr. Smartypants, then why did Mr. Angelino ask us to do it?"

"He was trying to get you out of his hair!" Justin guffawed. He collapsed where he stood, and rolled around with laughter. "While you're

57

at it, you better keep an eye on the school! It might blast off for Jupiter any minute! Watching the cement! How dumb can you get?"

"We're earning points, and you're not," retorted Jessica, "so who's dumb?" ·

Justin scrambled up, and dusted off his huge raincoat. "When Mr. Smith is in handcuffs, we'll have more points than we know what to do with."

Jessica gazed toward the Hotel Dover. "Isn't that Mr. Smith's car?"

Justin wheeled. "No fair! I wasn't ready!" He began to run for the hotel, but tripped on the bottom of his coat and fell flat on his face.

"It's too late," said Margaret. "He's in his car already."

Justin looked up. The white Pontiac was heading their way. In a few seconds, it would be past and gone. His eyes fell on the red marker flag, which was stuck in the ground beside the cement tray. Without thinking, he snatched up the flag and ran out into the street.

"Stop! Construction! Cement! Whoa!"

"Justin, what are you *doing*?" cried Margaret.

Mr. Smith slammed on the brakes. The white car screeched to a halt. Behind it, the

Dover city bus was coming up fast. The driver geared down and braked hard. The bus squealed up behind the Pontiac.

WUMP!

It kissed the back bumper, jarring the car. With a *boing!* the trunk popped open.

Justin gawked. The trunk was jammed full of some kind of mechanical equipment. It could be evidence that Mr. Smith was the car thief! He whipped a small Polaroid camera out of the trench coat pocket, and ran around behind the car.

That was when Doctor Dog spotted him. Someone he recognized — *an old friend!* With a joyous bark, the Saint Bernard launched his big shaggy body straight up through the sunroof of the Pontiac. He descended on Justin from above, like a fuzzy dive bomber.

"Look out!" chorused all the passengers on the bus.

Doctor Dog came down with his hind legs on the pavement, his front paws draped over Justin's shoulders, and his great tongue lapping at Justin's face. Justin staggered backwards. The dog moved with him, yelping, licking, and wagging.

"Justin — *no-o-o-o-o!*"

Justin's heel hit the edge of the cement tray.

Then he and the Saint Bernard toppled full-length into the freshly mixed wet cement.

Mr. Angelino rushed over. "Girls! Girls! I thought you were watching the cement!"

"Look what you've done to my dog!" bellowed Mr. Smith.

"Help!" gurgled Justin, crawling sloppily out of the tray. He was completely covered in gray muck. "Quick! Somebody hose me down before it hardens, and I have to stay like this forever!"

Doctor Dog hopped out of the tray and gave himself a vigorous shake. Blobs of cement flew in all directions.

"I'm hit!" wailed Jessica, scrubbing a few specks from her T-shirt.

Justin pulled off his sunglasses and wiped the cement from his face. "Okay, Mr. Smith, what was that stuff in the back of your car?" he demanded.

Mr. Smith stared in sudden recognition. "You again?" He ran to the Pontiac and slammed the trunk shut. "Stay away from my car! Stay away from my dog! Stay away from my *life*!"

10

Handcuffs and Paw-Cuffs

As the students filed inside on Monday morning, Mr. Ortiz was inspecting the school's new front steps.

"What a terrible job!" he exclaimed. "It looks like there are *hairs* in the concrete!"

Margaret nodded wisely. "A Saint Bernard always sheds the most fur in April."

The principal was taken aback. "What Saint Bernard?"

"The one Justin fell in the cement with."

GOOD DEED CONTEST

GROUP	I	II	III	IV	V	VI	VII	Z
POINTS	16	7	10	9	8	11	8	−20

"Zzzzz!"

Justin hardly heard the class's buzzing. He was concentrating on the Polaroid photograph of the contents of Mr. Smith's trunk. At least, that was what it was supposed to be. What the picture really showed was Doctor Dog in full flight, descending from the sky. Only in one tiny corner was there a glimpse of Mr. Smith's mysterious equipment.

Justin leafed through *101 Detective Tips.* There were pictures of standard burglar tools, but nothing matched what was in Mr. Smith's trunk. And there sure weren't going to be any new photographs. Justin's camera was now part of the front steps of the school — encased in cement.

All morning Justin couldn't concentrate on anything Mr. Carter was saying. His mind could only see the evidence that had gotten away. He pictured Mr. Smith in handcuffs (and Doctor Dog in paw-cuffs) being locked in the county jail. Or even the state prison. What if Mr. Smith was the mastermind of a national network of criminals, wanted by the FBI? Catching him would be a good deed for the whole world! Justin might even get to go on TV! They'd give him a medal. And the president himself would take the three Z's to Tidal Wave Water Park, and go with them on Dunk Mountain! Justin's dad could lend the president a bathing suit just in case he forgot to bring his own. They looked about the same size.

And the good deed points! It had to be worth thirty — maybe forty — who could tell? If Mr. Ortiz got his car back, maybe even . . .

"*Fifty!*" he cried out.

Mr. Carter was looking down at him with disapproval. "No, Justin. Two times three is *not* fifty."

Two rapid-fire spitballs caromed off Justin's chin. "Nice guess, Einstein," hissed Byron Bigelow.

Justin came to life and noticed that the class was playing a times-tables game. The two finalists were Margaret and Jessica. Didn't it figure? They totally stunk at good deeds, but here they were, wasting all their energy on something useless!

He sat a little taller in his chair. At least one of the three Z's knew what was important.

With kindergarten field day coming up on Friday, the three Z's put Harvey, Nicolette, and Seth back into training.

The kindergartners loved it. Harvey was a natural athlete, a speedster, and a three-legged expert. Nicolette couldn't resist a challenge. She was a fierce competitor, sack race champ, and tee-ball home-run queen. And Seth was so thrilled nobody was going to beat him up that he was always willing to give a hundred and ten percent. He also had an uncanny sense of balance that made him unbeatable at the egg-and-spoon race.

Harvey's older brother didn't even have to wait around after school anymore. Kevin had managed to get himself a week of detentions. He now munched on milk and cookies in the punishment room.

"See if you can get them to switch back to chocolate chip," he informed Justin. "These sugar cookies are gross."

"Maybe you should go on a diet," Justin suggested. "You've been getting kind of fat from all these snacks."

In answer, Kevin took a huge bite. "Do you like seafood?" he mumbled. Suddenly, he opened his mouth wide, revealing the chewed-up cookie. "See? Food!"

"Yecch!" exclaimed Justin, slinking off to find his kindergarten team.

After practice, Justin was surprised to see his mother's car parked across the street. Trevor sat beside Mrs. Zeckendorf in the passenger seat. They were probably on their way home from the doctor's office. Trevor had a cold again.

Justin ran up and scrambled into the back seat.

"Where were you?" demanded his mother. "I looked all over the school."

"I'm an After-School Club volunteer." He had to hold himself back from adding: *Who's building the five-year-old mega-stars of the world.*

Mrs. Zeckendorf pulled out into traffic. "Justin, your brother is having his tonsils taken out on Saturday. The doctor thinks that will keep him from getting sick so often."

"You get to eat tons of ice cream," added Trevor.

"Great, Trev," mumbled Justin, but he wasn't really paying attention. Trevor's life was all tonsils and cough syrup, Kleenex and Vicks VapoRub, aspirin and nose drops. An Idea Man had to think big — kindergarten field day, the Good Deed Contest, and Tidal Wave Water Park!

The hours of practice paid off. By Thursday afternoon there was no question. Harvey, Nicolette, and Seth were the Number One team for kindergarten field day.

Even Margaret was impressed. "I've got to hand it to you, Justin. I thought the kids would hate it! This is a *real* good deed we're doing!"

"Too bad there's no, like, Olympics for five-year-olds," said Justin. "Think how many points *that* would be!"

"All I know is I better not get hit with the ball," warned Jessica. "My Gregory Ashford audition is Saturday, and there's no way the swelling would go down on time."

"Well," joked Justin, "maybe Clorinda would look good with a black eye."

"That's so funny I forgot to laugh," Jessica told him. "We should have left you in the cement."

Justin blew his whistle. "What's the word?"

"Victory!" chorused the three kindergartners, making the V sign with their fingers.

"Right!" cheered Justin. "Now, remember, tell your moms you need carbohydrates for dinner tonight. And go to bed early."

"See you tomorrow!" waved Margaret as the team scurried back into the school. She turned to Justin. "What a great bunch of kids! Really cute, too."

"Cute, shmute," scoffed Justin. "They're points in the bank. They're going to massacre the competition."

Margaret scowled at him. "When you look at

them, you don't see human beings. You just see stupid points!"

"More than that," Justin replied. "I see Dunk Mountain. I see Splasherooski Whirlpool-o'-Fun. I see the president in my dad's bathing suit."

Jessica stared at him. "You're weird!"

Margaret frowned. "There's just one thing that bothers me. Mr. Carter hasn't said a word about us and kindergarten field day."

"That's the best part," Justin chuckled. "Nobody else knows, so we're the only ones who trained a boffo team."

"But what if Mr. Ortiz changed his mind?" Margaret persisted. "What if we're *not* in charge of kindergarten field day. What if we did all this for nothing?"

The look of horror on Justin's face proved that even an Idea Man doesn't always think of everything.

11

Kindergarten Field Day

Friday was a cool, brisk day, but Justin was sweating all the same. The kindergarten class was heading out for field day, yet there was still no word from Mr. Carter.

"Class, take out your geography homework," said the teacher.

What? No! Justin craned his neck to look out the window. Harvey, Nicolette, and Seth were doing the special warm-up exercises *he* had taught them.

He caught a nervous look from Margaret. The other two Z's were blaming this on him. If they were cut out of field day, all those hours of practice would be for nothing! Margaret would scream about all the real good deeds they could have been doing. Then Jessica would start in about wasting rehearsal time for her stupid audition. Oh, no — Justin would never hear the end of it!

Mr. Carter walked around the room collecting the papers. "I'll mark these tonight, and you'll have them back tomorrow," he told them. "But right now I've got some special news. As part of the Good Deed Contest, our class is going to supervise — "

"Ya-*hooooo!*" Justin was out of his chair, celebrating. He did a wild dance around his desk, chanting, "Yes! Yes! Yes!"

Mr. Carter stared him down. "What are you so excited about? I haven't said anything yet!"

Blushing to the roots of his blond hair, Justin took his seat. "Oh, right."

Even the spitball from Byron Bigelow didn't dampen his mood. Kindergarten field day was *on.*

Justin was triumphant as Ms. Dollop, the kindergarten teacher, lined up her students in alphabetical order.

"Okay, class," announced Mr. Carter. "A to Z."

The three Z's arranged themselves at the end of the line. They stood directly across from Seth, Nicolette, and Harvey.

"What an Idea Man!" whispered Justin, elbowing Margaret and Jessica in the ribs.

"Bug off! My audition is tomorrow!" hissed Jessica.

Margaret was glowing. "It's really working

out! You may not be so stupid after all!"

Then the two teachers began pairing students — *from opposite ends of the line!* Mr. Carter started off with Group 1. But Ms. Dollop sent Seth, Nicolette, and Harvey over to Byron Bigelow and his partners.

"Wait a minute!" Justin leaped forward. "No fair!" He pointed to Seth, Nicolette, and Harvey. "They should be *our* group!"

Mr. Carter stared at him. "Why?"

"Because they're at the back, and *we're* at the back," Justin explained.

"So?"

"So you can't mix back and front."

"That's just silly," said Ms. Dollop.

"But we've been training them for two weeks!" blurted Margaret.

Harvey pointed at Margaret. "You *told*! You said we couldn't tell!" He turned to Justin. "She *told*!"

"Wait a minute," said Mr. Carter sternly. "Nobody knew about this. Have you been snooping?"

"No. Yes," Justin admitted. "A little. Hardly at all."

"Well, let this be a lesson to you," said Mr. Carter. "The whole point of the Good Deed

Contest is to help others, not to win by hook or by crook."

Margaret was a good sport. "Oh, well," she called to Harvey, Nicolette, and Seth. "Have a great day! Good luck in the events — "

Justin stared at her as though she had a cabbage for a head. "Are you nuts? Don't wish *them* luck! They're the enemy!"

"Oh, Justin, you're such a baby!" she said in disgust. "How can you say that after all the fun we've had with them? Those little kids are our *friends*!"

"Thank you, Miss Goody-Two-Shoes!" Justin snorted. He sidled up to Harvey. "There's been a change of plan," he whispered. "The new strategy is to *lose* at everything. Got it? Not win — *lose*!"

"No way!" cried Harvey. He turned to Seth and Nicolette. "What's the word?"

"*Victory!*" they chorused.

"Winning isn't everything — " Justin managed.

"Hey, Dorf-head!" barked Byron. "Get away from my group!"

The three Z's ended up with Alita Baker, Becky Daniels, and Derek Bigelow.

Derek was Byron's little brother. "My big

brother says you three Z's are jerks," he announced. "Zzzzz!"

"We can still win," said Justin through clenched teeth. "We've got a great group here! What's the word?" he prompted.

"My big brother says I don't have to do what you say," Derek informed Justin.

Alita scratched at the bright-red rash on her cheek. "I might be getting the chicken pox," she announced. "My three brothers all have it."

"I've never had chicken pox!" cried Jessica, hiding behind Justin and Margaret.

"Okay," said Margaret. "The first event is the egg-and-spoon race."

"Too bad," said Becky mildly. "I can't run."

"That's all right," Margaret explained. "If you run, you'll drop the egg. You just walk fast."

"I can't do that, either," Becky replied. "I have Clumsy Child Syndrome. I also can't jump, throw, or catch."

It was the truth. Becky didn't last one step in the egg-and-spoon race. Alita might have done better, but she reached up to scratch her rash with her spoon hand. This hurled the egg back over her shoulder, where it splashed on Justin's shoes. Derek was the only one to reach the finish line, but he was dead last.

Seth, Nicolette, and Harvey came in first,

second, and third, capturing all the ribbons.

"What's the word?" prompted Byron Bigelow.

"Victory!" cheered the winners.

Justin was purple with rage. "Did you hear that? *Byron* is using *our* slogan! And it's *working!*"

Margaret was jumping up and down, cheering her former team.

Derek Bigelow was not a good loser. "This is all your fault!" he accused Justin. "Why do I have to be on the Z's team?" Then he threw a major temper tantrum, complete with crying, kicking, and screaming. By the time Justin had hauled him to the washroom and cleaned him up, Harvey, Nicolette, and Seth each sported four prize ribbons. A kindergarten field day sweep was on.

Justin could take it no longer. He roared his outrage to the skies.

"I can't stand it!" he cried. "It wouldn't be so bad if our plan was lousy! But to have everything work *perfectly* — for Byron Bigelow — that — that — "

"Don't say bad things about my big brother!" sniffled Derek.

Things only got worse for the three Z's. By the leap frog relay, Alita was coming out in

73

spots. Margaret had to take her to the school nurse. She came back alone.

"Alita has a fever," she reported.

"Well, that's just great!" Justin exploded. "Not only did we train Byron's team to slaughter us — now we've only got two guys!"

"Guess again," put in Jessica, pointing across the field. There was Derek, sprinting at top speed for home.

"He can't just *leave*!" Margaret exclaimed. "This is school!"

Justin was disgusted. "Who cares? Nobody will ever know the difference."

"All right!" bellowed Ms. Dollop. "Everybody line up with your team for roll call!"

12

The Home Run Queen

Byron Bigelow put on a big act, pretending to be worried about his younger brother.

"He's only a little kid!" he sobbed. "He's not even allowed to cross the street by himself! What if he gets run over by a car?"

"There, there," soothed Mr. Carter. "Your mother is bringing him back. He's safe and sound."

"I can't believe the Z's let him get away!" Byron blubbered. "I was so scared! They should get more negative numbers!" Byron winked at the three Z's.

"Did you see that?" cried Justin. "He isn't worried! He's faking the whole thing!"

"How dare you say that!" scolded Ms. Dollop.

"You certainly *will* lose points for this," said Mr. Carter sternly. "It was your job to watch Derek. Instead, you were scheming — as usual! I'm very disappointed in all three of you."

Margaret studied her sneakers in total misery. It was the first time in her entire life that she had disappointed a teacher.

By the time Mrs. Bigelow brought Derek back to school, only the tee-ball game was left for kindergarten field day. The runaway was immediately sent to the office.

"But it wasn't my fault!" Derek whined to Mr. Ortiz. "It was the Z's! *They* made me do it!"

"They'll get their punishment when the time comes," promised the principal, ushering Derek inside the school.

"We're getting blamed for *everything!*" exclaimed Margaret in horror.

"Mr. Ortiz is a good principal, but he sure isn't very smart," commented Justin. "I mean, Derek is in trouble because he ran *away* from field day. If you want to punish him, you should make him *play*, not kick him out!"

"Let's just get through this and go home!" sighed Jessica. "I've got a lot of rehearsing to do tonight."

"Justin," called Mr. Carter. "You're holding up the tee-ball game. Take Becky to the outfield."

"But, sir!" Justin protested. "Tee-ball is the last game of field day — our only chance to *not stink* in at least *one* thing! Couldn't she play something important, like first base or short-stop?"

The teacher was angry. "We're not here to teach your poor sportsmanship to the kinder-garten!" He pointed. "Outfield."

The three Z's led Becky to her position.

"Okay, kid," Justin told her. "It's all up to you."

Becky looked nervous. "To *me*?"

"If you don't star in this game," said Justin, "we can kiss Tidal Wave Water Park good-bye."

"But I don't star in anything," Becky explained. "I have Clumsy Child Syndrome."

"Hey, look," said Margaret. "Nicolette's up first." She waved.

"Whoop-dee-doo," muttered Justin. All at once, it hit him. *Nicolette was the home run queen!*

He grabbed Becky by the arm and began dragging her deeper into the outfield. "Hurry up!"

Becky was mystified. "Why?"

KAPOW!!

Nicolette swung mightily, and the ball launched off its tee like a rocket to the moon. It streaked up and away, disappearing in the bright April sunlight.

"Deep center!" cried Justin.

77

Becky ran like a dancing ostrich, her skinny legs pumping. Her arms flew in all directions as she moved. Justin was hot on her heels.

Nicolette was rounding second base before the ball started on its way down.

Justin craned his neck. "See it?"

"I can't catch," Becky explained patiently. "I have Clumsy Child — "

"There! There!" Justin interrupted. "It's coming down!"

"Be careful!" called Margaret. "You're almost at the road!"

It was true. The ball was going to land in the street — *off* school grounds. It was a home run. Unless —

At the last second, Justin grabbed Becky under her arms, and hoisted her high over his head.

"Catch it!"

Desperately, Becky reached up, and the ball thumped into her mitt. But before she could close her glove, Justin threw up his arms in victory.

Becky went down like a sack of oats. The ball bounced off Becky's head first, then Justin's head, and rolled into the street.

Nicolette crossed home plate, while her teammates cheered, *"Victory!"*

Justin helped Becky back to her feet.

She scowled at him. "That wasn't my fault," she said accusingly. "I think you have Clumsy Child Syndrome, too."

"I'll get the ball." Justin blushed. He crossed the street and bent down to pick it up.

And froze.

It was the white Pontiac — Mr. Smith's car! It was parked by the shipping entrance of the old Gunhold warehouse. Mr. Smith and two other men were carrying large pieces of equipment inside.

Heart pounding, Justin scooted behind a mailbox.

"Starting tomorrow," Mr. Smith was saying, "we'll bring them all in here."

Bring them all? Bring *what* all?

The stolen cars!

13

Police Raid

Crouched behind the mailbox, Justin shook with excitement. He had to hold himself back from jumping up and cheering. This was it! If the three Z's could arrest Mr. Smith here — *today* — nobody would care about the field day foul-ups! The Good Deed Contest would be over, and Tidal Wave Water Park would be theirs!

"Justin!" called Mr. Carter's voice. "Where did you go?"

Oh, no! Mr. Carter was looking for him! Justin made himself small behind the mailbox.

Mr. Smith was talking again. "Cal, are you ready to make them over?"

Justin peered out. The man called Cal was grinning. "Their own mothers won't recognize them."

Justin frowned. Now, what could that mean? He thought back to *101 Detective Tips*. All at once he had the answer! Cal was in charge of repainting the stolen cars and changing their license plates so they wouldn't be recognized! It all fit together! Only — what was the third man's job?

Mr. Smith provided the answer. "Okay, Larry, we'll need you when the shooting starts — "

Shooting! The word echoed in Justin's brain. These were armed and dangerous criminals!

Justin's mind raced. He had to notify the police — but he couldn't risk being spotted by Mr. Smith —

Suddenly, Justin was grabbed by the shoulder and hauled to his feet. Mr. Carter glowered down at him. The teacher's face was an unhealthy shade of purple.

"Are you crazy, Justin?" he bawled. "What do you have to say for yourself?"

As Justin searched his mind for an answer, there was a familiar bark. From the back seat of the Pontiac, Doctor Dog had just noticed Justin — his best friend in the whole world — *in trouble!*

The big Saint Bernard exploded out the open window and launched himself at Mr. Carter. Teacher and dog crashed heavily to the sidewalk.

"Don't worry, sir!" cried Justin. "I'll send for

help!" He sprinted down the street and hurled himself into a phone booth, pushing 9-1-1.

"Hello? Police? If you want to catch the car thieves, come to the old Gunhold warehouse!" As an afterthought, he added, "And when you're done, could you please get the killer dog off my teacher?"

"Come on, Doctor Dog," pleaded Margaret. "Get off Mr. Carter!"

Try as they might, Margaret, Jessica, and Becky couldn't pull the Saint Bernard off the teacher's stomach.

"Whose dog is he?" panted Mr. Carter.

"Mr. Smith's," said Jessica.

"Who?"

"He's this guy Justin thinks is the car thief," Jessica explained.

Mr. Carter was wide-eyed. "Why would Justin think that?"

"Justin wants to catch the car thieves for the Good Deed Contest," Margaret admitted. "Mr. Smith is his suspect."

The teacher thought back to *101 Detective Tips*. "I *knew* that book meant trouble!"

Justin came running up. "Margaret! Jessica! Becky! Get away from that dog! He could maul you to death!"

"For the billionth time, Doctor Dog is *not* a killer!" exclaimed Margaret, rolling her eyes. "He only jumped on Mr. Carter to protect *you!*" she told him. "Face it, Justin, this dog loves you."

On cue, Doctor Dog hopped off of Mr. Carter and trotted over to lick Justin's hand.

Mr. Carter stood up and dusted himself off. When he looked at Justin, his face was a thundercloud. "Justin Zeckendorf," he said quietly, biting back rage, "I hope you have a very, very, *very* good explanation for your behavior today."

"If you'll wait a minute, you'll understand everything," Justin promised.

"I'm sick and tired of your games — " the teacher began.

That was when they heard the sirens.

Six police cars screeched around the corner. They pulled up in front of the old Gunhold warehouse. A platoon of uniformed patrolmen poured out and surrounded the entrance.

The captain spoke into an electric megaphone. *"Attention, you people in the warehouse,"* his voice boomed all through the neighborhood. *"We have you surrounded! Throw down your weapons and come out with your hands up!"*

A bewildered Mr. Smith inched his way out of the warehouse. The other two men followed, their hands on their heads. Doctor Dog trotted over to stand with his owner.

Justin decided the time was right. He bolted onto the scene. "Hey, Officer — "

"Come back here!" hissed Mr. Carter.

"I'm the guy!" Justin raved on. "The guy who called up!" He pointed to Margaret and Jessica. "These are my partners. Do you think you could write a letter to our teacher about this?"

"Stand back!" ordered the captain. He frisked Mr. Smith and pulled out a leather wallet. He looked at the driver's license and turned pale. "This man isn't a car thief!" he blurted. "He's Gregory Ashford, the famous movie director!"

Jessica gasped in horror.

"That's impossible!" cried Justin. He turned to the policeman. "I heard them! They were talking about *shooting*!"

"With a *camera*!" Gregory Ashford exploded. "We videotape our auditions so we can watch them again!"

"You're lying!" Justin accused. He pointed to the man called Cal. "You talked about 'making them over' — "

"That's *makeup,* you dodo!" Jessica exclaimed.

"But all the equipment — " Justin managed.

The director pointed inside the warehouse. "Cameras, lighting, sound."

Justin played his trump card. "Okay! If you're this Gregory guy, why do you go around calling yourself Smith?"

"Because I like my privacy!" snapped Gregory Ashford. "And it was working out just fine — until you rotten kids showed up! I never want to see you three again as long as I live!"

"But what about me?" Jessica blurted. "I have an audition tomorrow! At two-fifteen! Sharp!"

The director's eyes blazed. "As of this minute, it's canceled! You're *out!* Got it? Washed up! Finished!"

Jessica turned deathly white. Her lower lip quivered. Her eyes misted over. For a moment, she looked like a baby about to bawl. Then — all at once — the tears were gone. She hurled herself at Justin's throat, shrieking a battle cry, *"I'll kill you!"*

14
Starting from Scratch

GOOD DEED CONTEST

GROUP	I	II	III	IV	V	VI	VII	Z
POINTS	21	12	13	11	11	16	11	−30

Justin moped around the house all weekend. The laughter of the other groups still rang in his ears. Kindergarten field day had been the icing on the cake of disaster. And Tidal Wave Water Park was now totally out of reach.

He tried telephoning his partners.

Margaret was bitter. "How-dare-you-call-me-Justin-Zeckendorf-after-what-you-did-you-humiliated-us-in-front-of-the-whole-town-I-can-never-show-my-face-again!" And she hung up.

Jessica was more to the point. "Drop dead, creep!"

Click!

Justin felt terrible. Sure, Jessica drove everybody crazy with her acting career. That was only because it meant so much to her. Now Justin had ruined her big chance. And Margaret. She tried *so* hard to be the best at everything. And, yes, that was kind of goofy. But it also explained why she was so *mad* at Justin for making idiots out of all of them. How would he ever square things with the girls?

Depressed, Justin wandered through the house. He listened to the loud slurping noises from the kitchen. Trevor had just come back from having his tonsils out. Now he was trying to suck back an entire half gallon of ice cream in one gulp.

Justin sighed. Trevor was the lucky one. He had coughed and wheezed his way through the whole Good Deed Contest. Now his biggest worry was "Vanilla Fudge or Chocolate Pecan Cocoa Crunchola?" Not stolen cars, or killer dogs, or movie directors, or where to get a bathing suit for the President of the United States so he could go on Dunk Mountain. Being an Idea Man was a heavy burden.

He dragged his feet to the front porch and slumped down heavily on the steps. There he sat, head in hands, looking gloomily out at the world.

He felt an arm around his shoulders. When he looked up, his mother was sitting beside him. Her face was full of concern.

"What's the matter, Justin?"

"Oh, everything," Justin moaned. "The Good Deed Contest is down the drain; Mr. Carter hates me; the whole class thinks I'm nuts; Margaret won't talk to me; Jessica says I ruined her acting career — " He looked at her tragically. "And the worst part is — they're probably right."

His mother smiled sympathetically. "Maybe you should tell me what's happened."

Justin was so upset that he found himself confessing. And once he got started, it was like a flood — Mrs. Milarchuk, the raffle, the McClintocks' living room, his investigation of the stolen cars, Doctor Dog and the cement, kindergarten field day . . .

"How was I supposed to know that Mr. Smith was really a big movie director in disguise?" he finished.

Mrs. Zeckendorf gave him a big hug. "Oh, Justin, I know *exactly* what happened to you. You were an Idea Man, weren't you?"

Justin hung his head. "My life is over. What can I do?"

"I know," she smiled. "You can start from scratch. Pretend the contest is just beginning. There are plenty of good deeds to be done."

"It's no use," moaned Justin. "We're a million points behind. And, anyway, Margaret and Jessica won't be my partners anymore."

"This isn't about winning," said Mrs. Zeckendorf. "It's about trying. You have to prove to Mr. Carter and to yourself that you're as capable as anyone of doing a good deed."

Justin looked hopeful. "Maybe" — He brightened — "I know! I could build a giant satellite dish so everybody in town can get hundreds of TV stations for free!"

His mother smiled wanly. "No, no. That's an Idea Man good deed. I've got a real one for you. Wash the car."

" . . . and Ronnie Taylor baby-sat for his little sister last night. That's another point for Group Six."

Mr. Carter updated the scores on the chalkboard. "There. I think that's everybody."

"Not yet." Justin raised his hand.

"*You?*" hissed Byron Bigelow. "Fat chance!"

"Zzzzz," buzzed the class.

Mr. Carter was cautious. "Justin, are you sure this is a real good deed?"

Justin handed him a piece of paper.

Mr. Carter handled the note as if it were a hand grenade. He opened it at arm's length.

89

All at once, the teacher's face glowed with relief.

"It's from Mrs. Zeckendorf! Justin washed the car yesterday!"

This got a very sarcastic standing ovation from everybody except Margaret and Jessica.

"Well," announced Mr. Carter, "that's one point for our three Z's." He erased the −30 and wrote in −29. It got a big laugh.

Justin glanced at his partners. "What do you think?" he whispered, sitting back down.

"I don't think about *you* at all," Margaret told him.

Jessica would not even look in his direction.

That evening, Mrs. Zeckendorf arranged with Mrs. Chisholm next door for Justin to wash *their* car. The McClintocks were still touchy about the flood in their living room. They refused to let Justin lay a finger on their BMW. But the Wandells up the street at the foot of the hill were more than happy to use his services.

Tuesday morning at school, Justin presented Mr. Carter with two more notes.

GOOD DEED CONTEST

GROUP	I	II	III	IV	V	VI	VII	Z
POINTS	25	15	17	15	14	19	13	−27

Three spitballs ricocheted off Justin's nose.

"Keep polishing that chrome, Dorf-head!" sneered Byron Bigelow. "You wash a gazillion more cars, and we're tied for first place. Just one problem — today's the last day of April!"

But Justin wasn't interested in Byron Bigelow. He was intent on winning back the approval of his fellow Z's. They sat tight-lipped at their desks, looking straight ahead.

15

Hit the Brakes!

The good thing about washing cars, Justin thought as he scrubbed, was that it kept a guy busy. There was no time to think — not about your partners hating you. Not about making an idiot of yourself in front of the whole town. Not even about Tidal Wave Water Park, and how you won't be going — which meant the President couldn't go, either (unless he remembered to bring his bathing suit from the White House).

He squatted down to scrape the mud from the license plate. Well, even if his fellow Z's wouldn't talk to him, he sure was getting popular with Mom and her friends. Obviously, everyone loved a free car wash. Too bad the Good Deed Contest was almost over.

Then he heard it — quiet humming, and the squeak of a cloth polishing a clean window. Cautiously, he peered under the bumper. There, at the other end of the car, stood two pairs of sneakers.

Justin jumped up. Margaret was working on the windshield, while Jessica waxed the hood.

"You guys are back!" Justin cried joyfully."This is great — "

And Jessica thrust her polishing cloth straight into his mouth.

"Don't say a word, Justin Zeckendorf!" she said between clenched teeth. "This doesn't mean we forgive you."

Justin pulled the rag out of his mouth. "Then what *does* it mean?"

"It means we're being good sports," Margaret replied sternly. "It's the last day of the contest, and we're working together as a team."

"Even though some of us still hate others of us a lot," added Jessica.

They worked in silence. Triple action made the job go triply fast. They were quickly done with the Robinsons' Dodge, the Khans' Oldsmobile, and the Lees' Volvo.

Margaret collected all the letters from the grateful car owners. "This is a normal good deed," she lectured. "If we'd done this for the whole contest, we'd be in first place right now."

"And I could have auditioned for Gregory Ashford instead of arresting him," Jessica added bitterly. "I could have been Clorinda by now."

Justin hung his head. "I'm really sorry. Look, there's only one car left. Then the Cokes are on me."

"Whose car?" asked Margaret.

Justin pointed. "The Fowlers'. At the top of the hill."

They struggled with their buckets and squeegees up the steep slope.

The Fowlers weren't home, but a blue Buick was parked at the side of the road.

"Well," Justin mused, "my mom definitely set this up with Mrs. Fowler."

Margaret frowned. "Doesn't Mr. Fowler drive a Mazda?"

Justin shrugged. "Maybe this is *Mrs.* Fowler's car. Or a new car. See how shiny it is?"

Jessica decided it for them. "Let's do it. I'm definitely not carrying all this stuff up the hill again."

Margaret still wasn't sure. "Well, it's not parked *exactly* in front of the house. And if it's their car, why isn't it in the driveway?"

But Justin was already pouring soapy water on the front fender. He pulled out his cloth and began to scrub.

"Justin!" Margaret squealed suddenly. "You're ruining their car!"

Justin looked down. His cloth had rubbed away the car's blue color, revealing red underneath. He made a swipe across the hood. More red.

Jessica ran a finger along the trunk. A blue smudge came off on her skin. "Wet paint," she commented. "This isn't a blue car. This is a red car that someone painted blue."

Justin almost leaped out of his skin with excitement. "It's one of the stolen cars!" he gasped. "Don't you remember my book? The thieves change the color of the cars they steal so no one will recognize them!"

"Don't start that again!" seethed Margaret.

"Hmmm," said Jessica thoughtfully. "This is a Buick. Wasn't Mr. Ortiz's car a red Buick?"

Justin howled his triumph to the sky. "We did it! We did it! We did it! They said we were too young to solve crimes, but we did it!"

"Pipe down!" scolded Margaret.

"You know," said Jessica faintly, "if there really are car thieves around, we could be in danger."

As if on cue, a strange man with bright red hair and a red beard appeared at the front window of the house beside the Fowlers'.

"Hide!" rasped Justin.

The three Z's looked around desperately.

There were no fences, no bushes; there was no cover at all.

"The car!" ordered Justin. He threw open the passenger door, and the three Z's piled inside. They kept low to avoid being spotted through the windows.

"Do you think he saw us?" quavered Margaret.

Justin risked a look. Red Beard was coming down the walk toward the car. Behind him lurked a giant of a man, barrel-chested, with arms like tree trunks.

"We're in big trouble!" Justin announced gravely.

Margaret peeked. "Maybe they're not car thieves! Maybe they're just mad because we wrecked their paint job, and they'll tell Mr. Carter, and we'll get more negative numbers, but that's all!"

Jessica raised her head and stared in horror at the two approaching thugs. "I hate you, Justin Zeckendorf! First you ruin my career, and now you're getting me killed!"

Justin's heart pounded in his throat. The Idea Man in him was scrambling for a plan of escape. All at once, the perfect scheme came to him. But —

Wasn't it this Idea Man stuff that always got

him into the most trouble? Hadn't it landed him thirty points below zero, and made him the laughingstock of Dover? On the other hand, this was no silly school contest. This was real life, real danger —

"Hey, you kids!" bellowed a gruff voice.

Justin made his move. Twisting like a pretzel, he reached under the dash and released the emergency brake. Then he sprang up and shifted the car into neutral. The Buick began to roll backwards down the hill.

"Hey, come back here!" shouted the man with the red beard.

The principal's car picked up speed. Justin and Margaret looked back out the front window. The two car thieves were getting smaller and smaller at the top of the rise.

"We're saved!" cheered Margaret. "Now — how do we stop?"

Justin looked blank. "Stop?"

The Buick went free-wheeling through a red light and narrowly missed an ice-cream truck.

"Get out of the way!" Justin shouted through the window. He reached up and sounded the horn.

Lying flat on the floor, Jessica slammed the brake pedal with both hands. The speeding car slowed down a little.

"That's it!" cheered Justin. "Way to go, Jessica!"

"But — but — " stammered Margaret. She pointed out the front window in horror.

It was the two car thieves, coming up fast on a Honda motorcycle.

"Get off the brake!" howled Justin. "They're gaining on us!"

Mr. Ortiz's Buick hurtled backwards past Justin's house, past the school. It was gaining speed at an alarming rate. The lines on the street were just a blur.

"Call the cops!!" bellowed Justin out the window.

The Buick zoomed to the bottom of the hill and jumped the curb. They sideswiped a mailbox and sheared a fire hydrant off its post. A water spout shot up twenty feet. The principal's car didn't slow down.

The three Z's bounced all over as the Buick smashed a picket fence, plowed through a tulip bed, and flew the wrong way down a one-way street. Horns honked and brakes squealed as other cars swerved to get out of the way.

Justin and Margaret both saw it at the same time — the old Gunhold warehouse, right in their path.

"Hit the brakes!" cried Justin at top volume.

Jessica slammed down the brake pedal with all her might.

Inside the warehouse, the movie auditions were finally over. Gregory Ashford was depressed.

"Why did I ever come to Dover?" he mourned. "Three days of tryouts — *fifty-four* actresses! — and not one kid who could play Clorinda!"

Larry, the cameraman, put an arm around the director's shoulders. "Cheer up, boss. Have faith. For all we know, the perfect Clorinda is about to come right through that door."

C R A S H !!!

The runaway Buick smashed backwards into the warehouse, shattering the big wooden door into splinters. The crew dove for their lives. The car skidded across the floor and stopped, dead center.

The Z's scrambled out, dazed.

Gregory Ashford gawked. "It's those three kids again!"

The two car thieves roared their motorcycle in through the broken garage door.

The man with the red beard pointed. "There!"

The car thieves leaped off the Honda.

"Now, just a minute — " interrupted Gregory Ashford.

The barrel-chested man swept him out of the way as though he were a mosquito.

Red Beard ran to the runaway car and opened the trunk. He pulled out a suitcase. "Let's go!" he called to his partner.

"They're getting away!" cried Margaret.

Justin's mind raced. How could they stop the car thieves? His eyes fell on the silver key in the starter of the Honda. Without the key, that motorcycle wasn't going anywhere!

With a battle cry, Justin leaped at the Honda and yanked out the key.

"Grab that kid!" ordered Red Beard.

The two thugs advanced on Justin.

Justin backed up. *Help!* he shouted out the hole in the door.

His cry reached no passersby, but it *did* make it to the keen ears of Doctor Dog. With a bark of outrage, the Saint Bernard bounded onto the scene, ready to defend his dearest friend. Teeth bared, he flew through the air like Superman. He tackled Barrel Chest broadside, knocking him into Red Beard. The Saint Bernard landed on top of them, drooling and growling, a giant paw on each face.

The suitcase flew out of Red Beard's hand. It hit the floor and burst open. All at once, the air was filled with —

"*Money!*" chorused the three Z's.

It was true. Cash fluttered around the warehouse like confetti — all the profits from the stolen car ring!

"So *that's* why they were chasing us!" breathed Margaret.

"They didn't care about us, or even the car!" breathed Justin. "They were after the money they hid in Mr. Ortiz's Buick!"

A uniformed policeman rushed in through the hole where the garage door had been. "What's going on here?"

Justin pointed to Doctor Dog's victims. "It's the car thieves! Arrest them!"

The officer was wary. "Aren't you the kid who arrested Gregory Ashford? Who've you got this time — Walt Disney?"

Margaret ran over to the wreckage of the Buick. "This is really a red car! It was stolen from our principal!" She rubbed some blue paint off with her hand. "See?"

Justin addressed the thieves on the floor. "My detective book says the thieves never use a stolen vehicle for the getaway."

"They do when the real getaway car is in the

repair shop," complained Red Beard from under Doctor Dog. "My first day in town, I was driving along — *and a pair of ladies underwear blew in the window!* Right in my face! I swerved into a telephone pole."

"But why was there underwear just flying around in the air?" asked Jessica.

The thief was bitter. "Because some idiot left a suitcase in the middle of the road, and it got hit by a cement truck!"

Mrs. Milarchuk! Their very first good deed!

"Aha!" Margaret was triumphant. "Why did the underwear cross the road? *To stop the car thieves!"*

Gregory Ashford blew his stack. "Flying underwear! Car thieves! Lousy actors! Rotten kids! This town is one big insane asylum!" He pointed at Justin. "And *you're* the head inmate!"

Justin studied his sneakers in embarrassment. He was about to stammer an apology when Jessica stepped in front of him. She faced the director, her eyes blazing.

"How *dare* you talk that way about my friend Justin? You don't even know how excellent he is! He caught a ring of car thieves all by himself! He's an Idea Man! And you — you're a jerk!"

Gregory Ashford looked startled. "That's her! That's Clorinda!"

"My name is Jessica!" she interrupted angrily. "J-E-S — "

But the director was in raptures. "No — that's exactly the kind of fire and spirit that I need for the actress who plays Clorinda! I want you to be in my next movie!"

"Never!" stormed Jessica. "Not in a million years — "

Justin and Margaret each clamped a hand over Jessica's mouth. They looked up at Gregory Ashford, and chorused, "She'll take it!"

16

Heroes

The next morning, the headline of the Dover *Gazette* blazoned:

CAR THIEVES BEHIND BARS

Justin was bursting with pride. "What does it say about us?"

Margaret skipped to the end of the article. She read, " 'The arresting officer was assisted by three fourth graders from Spruce Valley Elementary School.' "

"That's *it*?" Justin exploded. "No names? No pictures? Nothing about how we risked our lives to lure dangerous criminals into the old Gunhold warehouse?"

"We didn't lure them," Margaret explained patiently. "We got trapped in a runaway car, thanks to you. And we're lucky to be alive."

"I wouldn't line my birdcage with this newspaper!" Justin raved. "What a rag! They leave out all the important parts!"

"Like what?" challenged Margaret. "How we took our principal's car and made it look like a pile of broken Christmas tree ornaments? Personally, I'm glad they left *that* out."

Jessica leaned over from her seat. "If it wasn't for last night," she beamed, "I wouldn't get to be Clorinda in Gregory Ashford's movie!"

Mr. Carter breezed in and went straight to the bulletin board. "Attention, everyone. The Good Deed Contest is over, and Group One is the winner, with twenty-five points."

Byron and his partners celebrated wildly.

There was a knock at the door, and Mr. Ortiz entered. "Boys and girls, I have some news that affects this class. The Chief of Police was just in my office."

"What did the Z's do this time?" piped Byron Bigelow.

"The Z's are heroes," the principal replied. "Yesterday they played a very big part in capturing the car thieves. Thanks to them, all the stolen vehicles have been returned to their owners." He looked miserable. "Except mine. My beautiful Buick had to go to the scrapyard. Anyway" — he tried to sound cheerful — "I'm awarding fifty Good Deed points to Justin, Margaret, and Jessica for their — uh — wonderful work."

Justin held his breath while Mr. Carter did the arithmetic on the bulletin board. Fifty points! Surely that would get the Z's out of the negative numbers and into the lead!

Byron Bigelow crossed his fingers, toes, and eyes, and chanted, "Jinx! . . . Jinx! . . . Jinx! . . ."

"Well," said Mr. Carter, "you were −27, plus 50 gives you a grand total of 23. A very big jump. And a close second place."

Justin deflated like a balloon. Second place.

"Ha, ha, ha!" laughed Byron Bigelow. "In your face! They gave you fifty points, and you still lost!"

"Byron, that will do," said Mr. Ortiz sternly.

"Sir! Sir! Oh, sir!" Margaret jumped up. "I forgot until this minute! Yesterday we washed three cars before we found the stolen one! I have the letters to prove it!"

Even Justin could do *this* math. Three more good deeds gave them 26 points. Group 1 only had 25.

"The Z's are the winners!" announced Mr. Carter.

"Dunk Mountain, here we come!" bellowed Justin, over the moon with happiness.

The three Z's celebrated, while the class gave them a round of applause.

Byron Bigelow was not clapping. "That's not fair!" he wailed. "You said *we* were the winners! It's a rip-off! The whole contest is fixed! You're all cheaters! I'm telling!"

Mr. Ortiz stepped forward. "That's enough, Byron!" he said sharply. "I'm going to take the first *and* second place groups to Tidal Wave Water Park this Saturday. No more poor sportsmanship, or you won't get to go!"

Byron sulked, but Justin beamed as the final scores went up on the board.

GOOD DEED CONTEST

GROUP	I	II	III	IV	V	VI	VII	Z
POINTS	25	16	18	17	15	20	14	*26*

17

The Mystery Package

The victory trip to Tidal Wave Water Park was set for Saturday. The whole Zeckendorf family was going along. Now that Trevor's tonsils were out, his constant sneezes and sniffles had finally stopped.

"It's kind of a rip-off," Justin admitted. "What's the point of winning the contest if I was going to get to Tidal Wave Water Park anyway?"

"But now that Trevor's okay, your family can go as often as you want," Margaret pointed out.

"Right," grinned Justin. "But this first trip is going to be the sweetest — because it came from the greatest comeback in Good Deed Contest history!"

For the first time ever, the three Z's all agreed on something.

The big day finally came. Justin was so excited, he was practically bouncing off the walls of the living room. His mother ordered him to sit down on the couch beside Trevor, Margaret, and Jessica.

"But I don't want to be late!" Justin whined.

"Late for what?" asked Mrs. Zeckendorf in exasperation. "The Park is open all day!"

Outside, Byron Bigelow and his partners waited with Mr. Ortiz in the principal's brand-new Buick. The winners from the other grades were already on their way. Everyone was ready. Everyone except —

"Dad!" Justin exploded. "What's taking so long?"

"I can't find my bathing suit!" his father called back.

All at once, Justin turned beet-red. "Oops."

"His dad's bathing suit!" Jessica exclaimed suddenly.

Margaret stared. "Justin, you *didn't!*"

In the Oval Office, the President was baffled by the strange package. Secret Service agents opened it. Everyone stared.

It was a faded pair of orange swimming trunks decorated with pictures of palm trees.

The Secretary of State found his voice first. "It — it must be a hoax, sir. What kind of clown sends the President a used bathing suit?"

"There's a note," said the President, beginning to read aloud. " 'Dear Mr. President, I *would be totally honored if you would be my guest at Tidal Wave Water Park in Dover. Meet me at Dunk Mountain at one o'clock, Saturday afternoon. Signed, Justin Zeckendorf, 4th Grade Good Deed Champion.*' "

The President checked his watch. It was 12:15. His meeting with the Canadian prime minister wasn't until six.

"Get me a helicopter," he said. With a wry smile he added, "And a towel."

About the Author

Gordon Korman has written over fifteen books for children and young adults, including three ALA Best Books for Young Adults: *Son of Interflux*, *A Semester in the Life of a Garbage Bag*, and *Losing Joe's Place*. His novel *The Twinkie Squad* was a selection of the Junior Library Guild. When Korman was twelve, he wrote his first book, *This Can't Be Happening at Macdonald Hall!*, about the adventures of two friends, Bruno and Boots. He published five other books by the time he graduated from high school, and has written five more books about Bruno and Boots, most recently, *Macdonald Hall Goes Hollywood*. His latest novel is called *The Toilet Paper Tigers*.

A native of Ontario, Canada, and a graduate of New York University's School of Dramatic Writing, Korman divides his time between Pompano Beach, Florida; Toronto; and New York City, and writes full time.